A DAY WITH A FIREFIGHTER

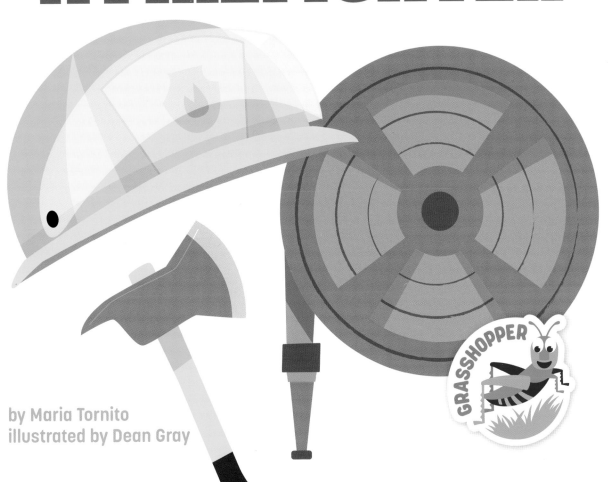

by Maria Tornito
illustrated by Dean Gray

GRASSHOPPER

Tools for Parents & Teachers

Grasshopper Books enhance imagination and introduce the earliest readers to fiction with fun storylines and illustrations. The easy-to-read text supports early reading experiences with repetitive sentence patterns and sight words.

Before Reading

- Discuss the cover illustration. What do they see?
- Look at the picture glossary together. Discuss the words.

Read the Book

- Read the book to the child, or have him or her read independently.
- "Walk" through the book and look at the illustrations. Who is the main character? What is happening in the story?

After Reading

- Prompt the child to think more. Ask: Have you ever met a firefighter? Would you like to?

Grasshopper Books are published by Jump!
5357 Penn Avenue South
Minneapolis, MN 55419
www.jumplibrary.com

Library of Congress Cataloging-in-Publication Data

Names: Tornito, Maria, author. | Gray, Dean, illustrator.
Title: A day with a firefighter / by Maria Tornito; illustrated by Dean Gray.
Description: Minneapolis, MN: Jump!, Inc., [2022]
Series: Meet the community helpers!
Includes reading tips and supplementary back matter.
Audience: Ages 5-8.
Identifiers: LCCN 2021000099 (print)
LCCN 2021000100 (ebook)
ISBN 9781636902135 (hardcover)
ISBN 9781636902142 (paperback)
ISBN 9781636902159 (ebook)
Subjects: LCSH: Readers (Primary)
Fire fighters–Juvenile fiction.
Classification: LCC PE1119.2 .T67283 2022 (print)
LCC PE1119.2 (ebook) | DDC 428.6/2–dc23
LC record available at https://lccn.loc.gov/2021000099
LC ebook record available at https://lccn.loc.gov/2021000100

Editor: Eliza Leahy
Direction and Layout: Anna Peterson
Illustrator: Dean Gray

Printed in the United States of America at Corporate Graphics in North Mankato, Minnesota.

Table of Contents

A Visit with Captain Reyes

Fire Captain Reyes is Owen's neighbor.

Today, she has invited Owen's family to the fire station!

"Let's go on a tour!" Captain Reyes says. "What would you like to see first?"

"The trucks!" says Owen.

5

Owen looks up. This fire truck has a ladder that stretches up high.

"That's called a ladder truck," Captain Reyes says. "It carries a lot of our tools."

"What do you need ladders for?" Owen asks.

"We climb them. We use them to save people from tall buildings," she says.

"What does this truck do?" Owen asks.

"This is a fire engine. It helps us put out fires," Captain Reyes says.

"It carries water, hoses, and more tools."

"I've seen this one driving! It lights up," says Owen.

"That's right!" Captain Reyes says. "The ambulance carries people to the hospital."

"We wear gear, like jackets and helmets," Captain Reyes says. "It protects us from fire. Want to try on some gear?"

"Yes!" Owen says.

"This is the break room. We rest and eat here," Captain Reyes says.

Owen waves to the firefighters.

16

Suddenly, the alarm rings.

"Fire at Fifth and Vine Street!" a loudspeaker booms.

"We have to go!"
Captain Reyes says.

The firefighters rush
to put on their gear.

They leap into the trucks.
Lights flash. Sirens sound.

"Be safe!" Owen calls.

"Maybe you'll join our crew
one day!" Captain Reyes
calls to Owen.

Quiz Time!

Which does Captain Reyes show Owen first at the fire station?

A. the ladder truck   **B.** the fire engine
C. the ambulance   **D.** the break room

Firefighting Tools

Owen saw these firefighting tools at the fire station.
Can you point to them in the book?

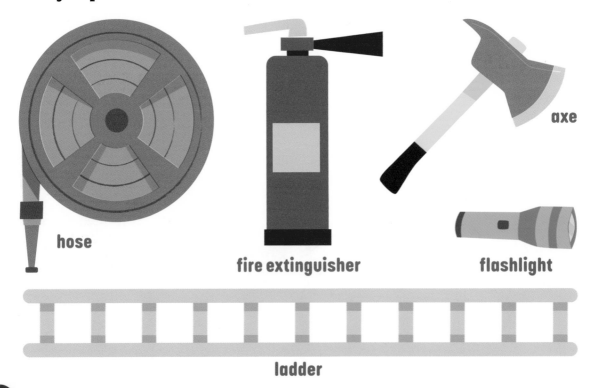

hose

fire extinguisher

axe

flashlight

ladder

22

Picture Glossary

alarm
A device with a bell, siren, or buzzer that warns of danger.

ambulance
A vehicle that takes ill or injured people to a hospital.

captain
The leader of a team.

fire engine
A large truck that carries pumps, hoses, ladders, and firefighters to a fire.

fire station
A building where fire trucks and engines are kept.

sirens
Devices that make loud, shrill sounds and are used as signals or warnings.

Index

To Learn More

FACT SURFER

Finding more information is as easy as 1, 2, 3.

❶ Go to www.factsurfer.com

❷ Enter "**adaywithafirefighter**" into the search box.

❸ Choose your book to see a list of websites.